THIS BOOK BELONGS TO

_____

For my daughter Skye, overcoming challenges everyday!

Thank you to my husband, family and friends
For believing in me!

For the mentorship and support I received
Thank you Andrew and Heidi x

Shy Skye Flies High!

Written and illustrated
Jo Blake

High in the treetops, in a jungle far away,
A young parrot sat and watched her friends play.
Laughing and screeching as they flew through the air.

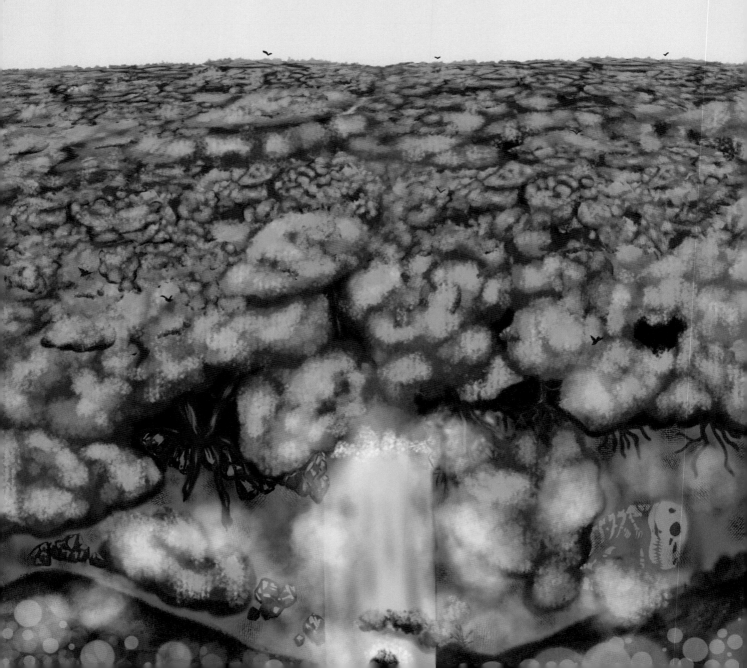

But still she just sat

and watched the world go by;

They wanted her to play but thought,
"Skye's just Shy!"

Her friends flocked around taking
Turns to fly by,

Skye gathered up courage,

tummy burning like fire!

She opened her wings, flying
Higher and higher.

They were so excited that Skye had joined in,
Their shrieks of laughter made a
Stupendous din!

Skye was having fun; she felt at ease.
Then, there was a rustle from within the
trees!

She felt a chill creep up her spine.
A shadow loomed over, but the sky looked
Fine?

With panic in her chest and rising dread,

She turned on her heels and away she fled!

From the tips of her toes to the top of her beak,
Finally Skye found the courage to **Shriek!**

So shocked were her friends to hear Skye shout,
They rushed to her side to ask,

A wide-eyed eagle had heard the commotion,
Scanning the treetops, looking for motion.
Into the canopy, they all swooped together.

To escape danger, they had to be clever!

"Hold very still,
keep your voices inside;
To outsmart this eagle,
We all have to hide!"

He hovered over the treetops.
There wasn't a sound. He looked for
Prey, but there was none to be
Found!

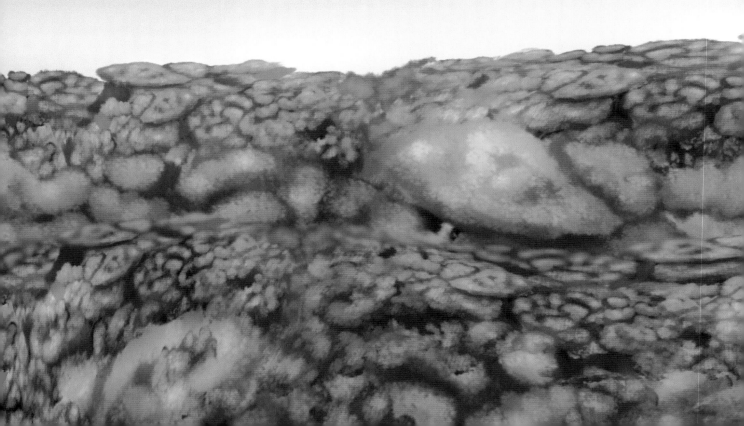

Hungry and fed up, time to move on,
As quick as he appeared, now he was
Gone.

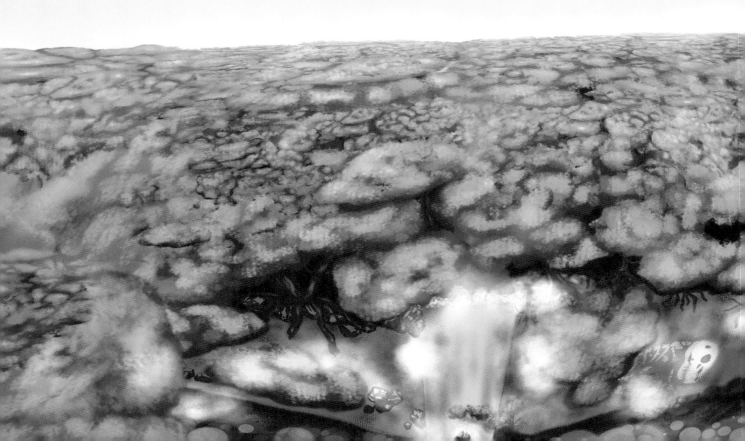

Out popped their heads one by one,
The danger had passed. Time to have
Fun!

The birds looked to Skye to lead the way.
As she was the cleverest,
And had saved the day!

High in the treetops, in a jungle far away,
A young parrot flew with her friends all day.
Laughing and screeching without a care,
Saying "Skye's so much fun!"

"Now she flies through the air!"

Jo Blake the Author and illustrator for
Shy Skye Flies High!
This is the first of her self-published works.

She has worked with Primary School children
teaching art and supporting their reading,
phonics and social emotional wellbeing.

When Jo isn't getting messy with paint, she
enjoys films, retro cartoons, gaming and walking
"Blue the dog"with her family; in the beautiful
Devon scenery.

You can find out more by following Jo Blake Art on facebook and instagram. wwwfacebook.com/joblakeart and
www.instagram.com/joblakeart
Shy Skye Flies High! Official fan group
https://m.facebook.com/groups/368423757848499/?ref=group_browse

Printed in Great Britain
by Amazon